TWITCHLAND

THE GRAPHIC NOVEL

Tim Mulligan

Illustrations by Pyrink

**THE WORLD OF WITCHLAND
BOOK 3**

Twitchland: The Graphic Novel
Copyright © 2025 by Tim Mulligan

This edition published by Highpoint Lit

For information, write to info@highpointpubs.com.

First Edition
ISBN: 979-8-9989720-0-3

Library of Congress Cataloging-in-Publication Data
Mulligan, Tim

Twitchland: The Graphic Novel

Summary: "When the local bats find their way into the buried tanks of radioactive and deadly toxic waste buried in the ground in Richland, Washington, home of the Hanford Nuclear Reactor cleanup site, a new type of monster is born. This third volume of the World of Witchland graphic novel trilogy finds our favorite family again left trying to understand and survive an unspeakably messy and dangerous cascade of events." — Provided by publisher.

ISBN: 979-8-9989720-0-3 (paperback)

Library of Congress Control Number: 2025910982

LGBTQ+ | Thriller | Horror

Cover and Interior Design by Pyrink
Project Management by Steisha Ponczoch
Manufactured in the United States of America

DANGER
Hazardous
Waste
Tanks
Chapter ONE

Hanford
Work Site

Well there's
Mr. Rico Suave.
Ready for
battle?

Hey.

One of these days, little man, we're going to have the same night off,
and I'm going to drag you out for some beers, and get you good and shit-faced.

That'll open you up. Maybe even get you laid... What do you think –
would you be up for that?

Oh I don't think so. Not much of a drinker.

That's what I'm saying. Let me and the other guys get you to loosen up a little bit...

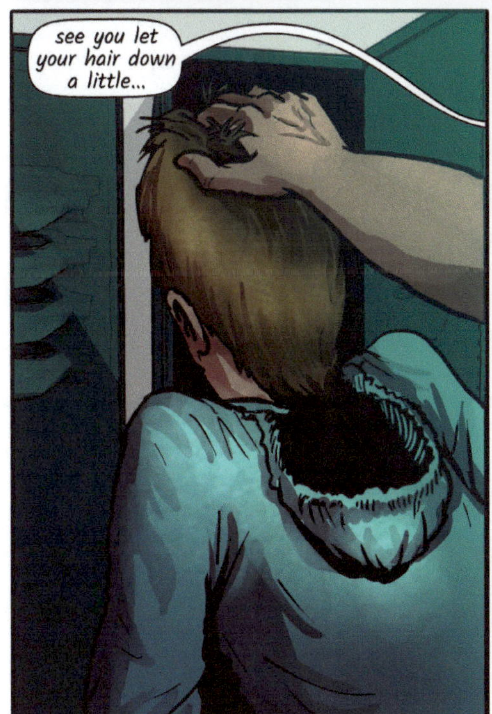
see you let your hair down a little...

You know, party it up. Richland style...

Well good night to you too!

Oh, and thanks Frank for such a nice invite...have a great night...

Fucking freak.

Stupid Tom.
Stupid, stupid, stupid.
Dumb stupid fuck head.

Oh sure, yeah, let's go out on the town. Beers. Get laid. Fuck you fuck you fuck you.

DANGER
Hazardous Waste Tanks

DANGER
Hazardous Waste Tanks

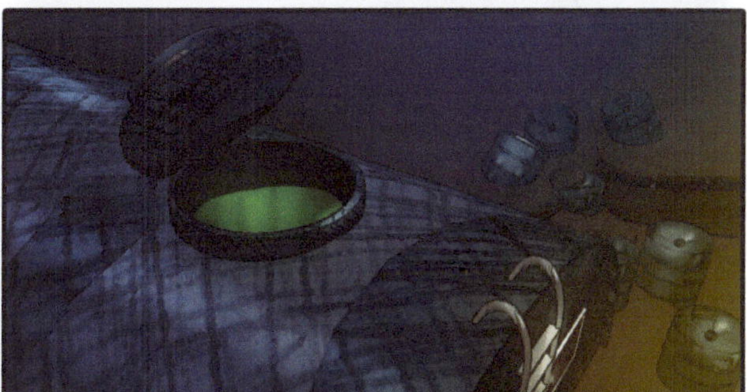

SPLASH

DANGER
Hazardous
Waste
Tanks

DANGER
Hazardous
Waste
Tanks

CLONK

THUD
THUD
THUD
THUD
DANGER Hazardous Waste Tanks
THUMP
THUMP

Thud

DANGER
Hazardous
Waste
Tanks

ardous
Waste
Tanks

DANGER
Hazardous
Waste
Tanks

DA
Ha

DANGER
Hazardous
Waste
Tanks

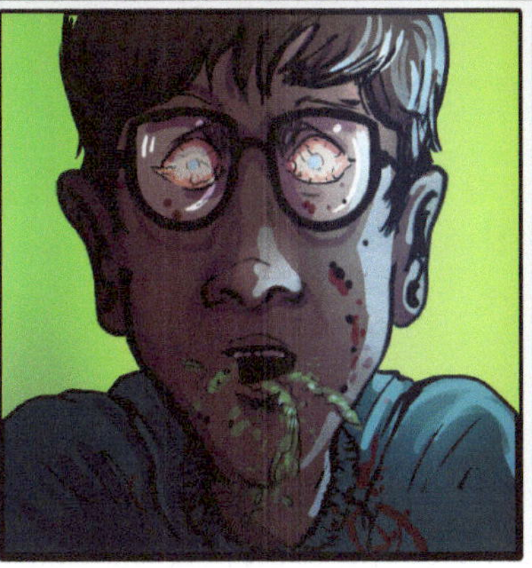
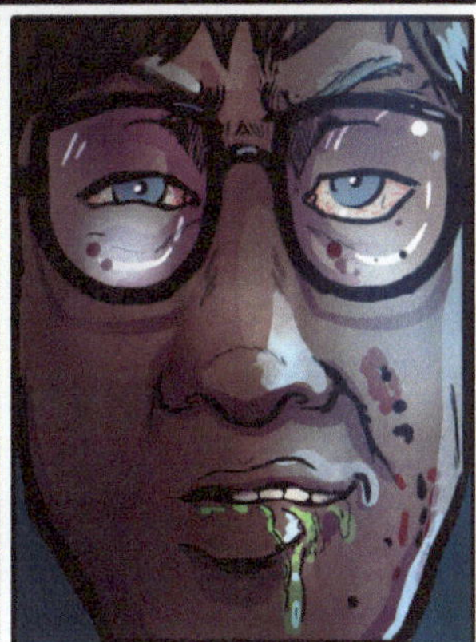

11

Let's go grab some beers at the Uptown. You down?

Hell yeah.
Have you ever known me to say no to that?
As soon as Freakazoid gets here, let's dip.

He's so fucking weird. You should have seen him last night.
I even tried to invite him out with us one of these nights — joking of course. You know what he said?

Let me guess..

No, I'm going to stay home with my cats, watch some gay porn and play with myself. Fucking dork.

Not even. Fucker didn't say anything.
Didn't even respond. Just walked on out, right past me. I couldn't –

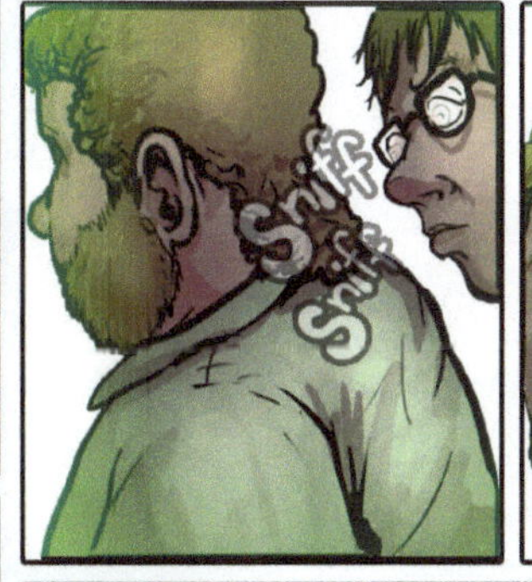

Sniff
Sniff

What the fuck? What are you think–

Dude... Tom... What's up?
You're not looking too hot.

Tom – are you like drunk or high or something?
You look really fucked up.

HAHA
HAHAHA

Little bitch just gets weirder and weirder. Who fucking cares.
Let's go drink.

WHAAAAAAAA

SPLASH
THUMP
SWISH
SPLISH
THUMP

LOCK

Meanwhile, across town...

Sam, dude, you're fucked up! You're so fucked up!
Fuck yeah I am. It's Friday night. Another Friday in Bitchland.

HAHA HAHA
HAHA

EEEK
EEEK

Wait, what the hell is that noise? Birds?

SWOOSH

EEKK
EEKK

Ahh
AAAH

Swoosh

A few blocks away...

Oh hey Van. Yup, got the pizza. I hope you got me a beer or two.
I'll be over in a few.
Wait, what?

Jesus fuck. Bats? What the hell is...

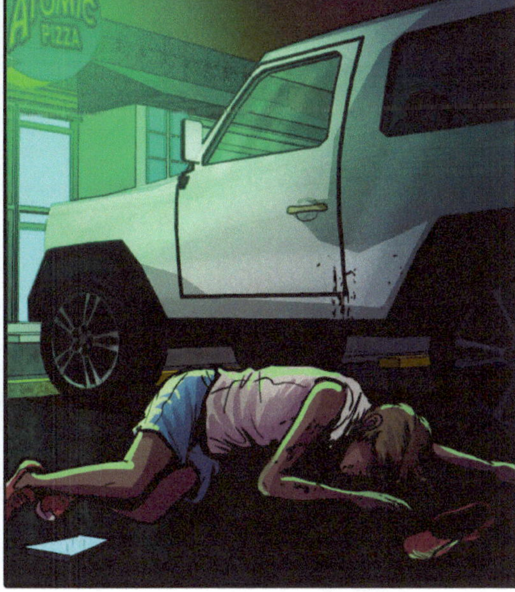

Van? The weirdest thing just happened...

What happened? Are you okay?

Hey, yeah. Sorry about that Van. I'll be right over.

Chapter THREE

Hey Ali girl, whassup? How's school going?

Well, I wouldn't worry about that. You always seem to pull out the killer grades in the end.
Just keep your pretty head in the game.
Tonight? Well...

Brett's finally making good on his promise and bringing over some pizza... we're having a good old-fashioned bros night.
I've been beefing up my football playoff knowledge.

Shit, I can name the top 8 teams even. Go Seahawks!

We're going to watch the game... eat pizza... and yes, I even bought non-alcoholic beer.
Yes, for both of us. Your darling dad's been good, I promise. No relapses. I'm in it to win it.

Like the Seabirds. I mean Seahawks. What? Oh, I know —
Brett thinks I'm getting him real beer. The last thing I need is to get caught providing alcohol to a minor.

This town would love to string this old queen up for something like that.

So it's O'Doul's for both of us.
Yes, I'm good. Just working, trying to stay busy...
and guess what your old Dad did... Give up?

No, I did not gain 50 pounds eating Spudnuts. The opposite, actually.

I'm taking golf lessons! It's actually kind of fun.
And you should see my cute golf outfits. Stretchy!
Jared's likely rolling in his grave.

He's probably here with me in this room at this minute, laughing at me. I even bought a —

AHHHHHH!

Jesus Christ Ali, Brett is standing here at the window like a zombie from The Walking Dead.
I should go — have a great weekend — don't study too hard. Go out.
Meet a boy.
Or a girl. Have fun. Bye —

Jesus Brett. What are you doing? Trying to kill me?
Like a goddam Peeping Tom. Peeping Brett.

Brett? Everything okay with you? You look a little out of sorts.
Wait, where's the pizza?

Brett... pizza? Did you already eat it on the way here?

Pizza. Shit. Be right back.

Brett, are you okay? What happened when you were on the phone?
It sounded like you were being attacked or something?

Attacked? What, no...
I just tripped and dropped my phone. I'm good. How are you. What's new?

I'm all right. Adjusting to life as a widower —
Ali calls me the Black Widow of Witchland — in this shitty town.
Still plugging away at the good old Spudnut Shack.
Spudnut Shack

Missing Ali, who I was just talking to — she says hello —
and who is of course knocking it out of the park at school.

What about you — how's the community college?
I hope you are getting enough time away from that nuclear reactor shitshow of a job to focus on your classes.

Brett, what's up with you?
Are you high?
What are you on?

No... not high. Just feeling a bit off. Not really myself. Maybe I'm catching something.
I should probably leave you alone, so you don't catch whatever I have.

Bullshit, you are not leaving.
We are having a boys' night, watching the playoff game, eating your pizza, and drinking fake beer.
I've been looking forward to this all week.

Brett, are you bleeding?
Is that blood on your shirt?

No, it's nothing. I'm fine.
You are not fine. Let me see this...

Fuck that Brett, this isn't nothing! What happened?
Is this your blood?
Sit down...

I'm fine Van. Look, I've got to go. Don't worry.
I'll be fine. Sorry about this. But I have to leave.

Hello? Dad?
Ali, it's me. Again.
Sorry. Ummm... something's up.
With Brett. I think... it's bad.

Chapter FOUR

Hey dickhead. Have a great fucking night.

What did you say to me?
Did you call me a dickhead?

I did.
I called you a dickhead, since that's what you are.

A pathetic, white trash dickhead. Now get the fuck away from me.

Well you little fuck –

What's happened to you? Jesus Christ.

Bounce.
Now.

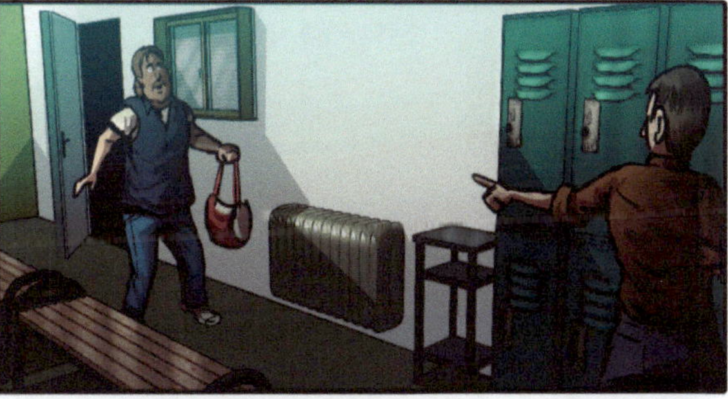

HANFORD
TOXIC
WASTE

SPLASH
WHISSH
SPLISH

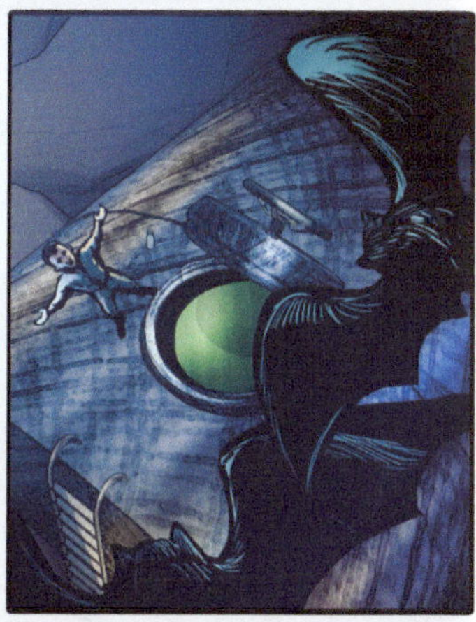

Chapter FIVE

EEEEEEECK!
The Spudnut Shack

Oh my God! What the?

Jennifer?
Jesus you bitch you almost gave me a heart attack.

40

Sorry, I just couldn't resist.
And you are literally the easiest person on Earth to scare.

That's not difficult in this fucking town.
You never know who's a witch, or a ghost, or whatever.
How are you? You look great! Can you sit down? Can I get you a Spudnut? Coffee?

That sounds lovely. I'll take a glazed, please!

So...what's new? I'm surprised you're still here, in this town.
I thought by now you would have taken your settlement check from Hanford and hightailed it out of here.
I can't imagine you want to stay after everything that happened...

Actually — and I know you will find this impossible to believe — I think I'm staying. At least for now. The money is enough to keep me afloat for awhile, and also get my daughter through school. Let's face it — it's cheap here. And I like my little house. So — I'm staying.

Well, that's music to my gay old ears.
Spudnut Shack
You're like my only friend around here!
Don't tell me you're planning on going back to work out there are you?

Welcome to Hanford
WHERE SAFETY COMES FIRST
Hell no, I took the package they offered me and left. I'm going to chill for a while, get my head back on straight. I might get my Master's, take up tennis —

Girl, take golf lessons with me! I just started! How fun would that be?
Golf?

Why not? Sign me up! And if you need a cashier here peddling potato donuts, I'm available.
Don't even say that unless you mean it. We'd be like the Alice and Flo of Witchland.
I can't believe it took a whole lot of bullshit and trauma for me to actually make a friend. And I get to be Flo, by the way.

It seems we are both at the same crossroads now.
I'm thinking of staying a while also, even with all the shit I've had to go through living here.
Thankfully those Hanford fuckers were quick to settle for what happened to Jared, and with that money I've got the house paid off, and Ali's school more than covered.
Honey, I can handle the homophobe stares from the army of Karens around here, and the redneck comments I continue to hear.

But what gets me is the danger — are we going to be okay here... health-wise? Are we crazy for staying?
That's the million-dollar question.

What I do know is that the cleanup out there is going to continue for decades.
Billions more dollars are being put into it. There are still over 50 million gallons of that toxic shit buried underground.

Whether or not they turn it into glass — or the latest crazy idea is concrete - this place is going to have a thriving economy for years. Will we be safe?

I think as long as they can keep it out of the river, and we don't go near the reactors, we should be okay.

How about this? Let's make a pact. Here, take my hands.

Let's stay until our beautiful daughters Ali and Linda get through college.
That's it. Then let's pick up and head out. Somewhere glamorous.

Yes, somewhere glamorous. Beverly Hills, or Montana. Park City.

Or a big city, like New York or San Francisco. Sounds dreamy. Until then, let's golf, eat donuts, play a little pickleball here and there, and watch our daughters thrive.

AAAHHHHHH
Oh my God, now what?
The Spudnut Shack

The Spudnut Shack

LOCK

Everyone, let's stay calm. Not sure what's happening outside. Let's give it a beat before I open the door again.
Don't worry, we have plenty of donuts and coffee!

The fun just keeps on a coming around here.
Good old Witchland.

Fucking Snitchland.

There's talk of another problem hitting these streets – the drug problem continues to grow here. This fentanyl shit is no joke.

I heard that too. It's so sad. Don't we have enough going on here with toxic waste, to add drugs to the mix? I read about four more overdoses last week.
AMBULANCE

Jesus, I remember the days when a big Saturday night involved some margaritas, maybe a line or two of coke, and if you're lucky someone will offer you a popper in the club.

Now these kids are mixing up that fentanyl shit with coke, making little tablets, and selling it like candy on the streets.
It's awful. And what that fucking little pill can do to you is anyone's guess – mixed with other shit, you never know. One pill could kill you.

I have to share something with you. It's Brett.
He came over the other night, and was high on something. And not only that – he had blood all over his shirt. He wasn't himself, kept looking around, twitching... girl, he was a hot mess.

No, not Brett. This fucking place. Fucking Twitchland.
Twitchland – good one. I called Ali. She's coming this weekend, to talk to Brett, see what's up. Ali to the rescue. Again.

Linda will be home this weekend also – let's all four get together? The girls can finally meet each other.
Your Communications major daughter and my Animal Science daughter – could make a formidable duo!
Yes, let's do that. I'll call you. I should go unlock the door... seems like whatever happened out there has calmed down.

CLICK

Sniff
Sniff
The Spudnut Shack

The Spudnut Shack

Sp
Sh

The Spudnut Shack

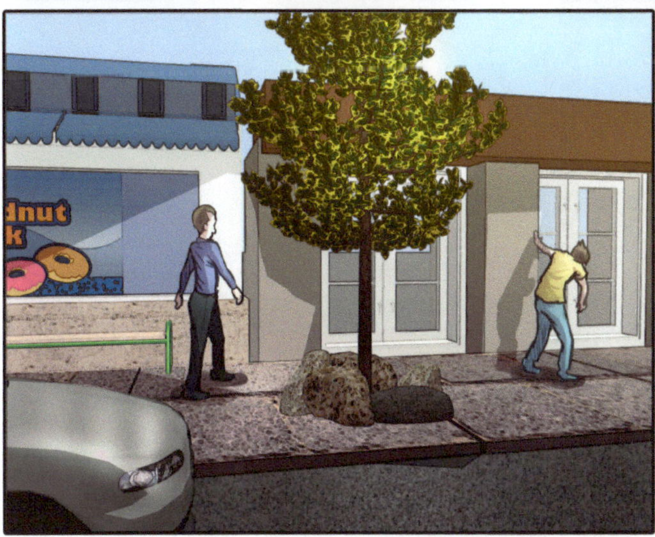

dnut
k

Hey. You.
Looks like you need some help.
Would you like...something to help with the pain... the fear... the twitches?

Yes. Please. Fucking yes. I need help.

Well then what are we waiting for. Let's go.

48

Chapter SIX

BOMBASTIC
CLUB

Dude, I can't. I'm freaking out. I'm so sick. I feel like I'm dying.
What do we do? These thoughts in my head... I feel like ripping people apart, I can't stop it. Fuck. What the fuck is happening to us?

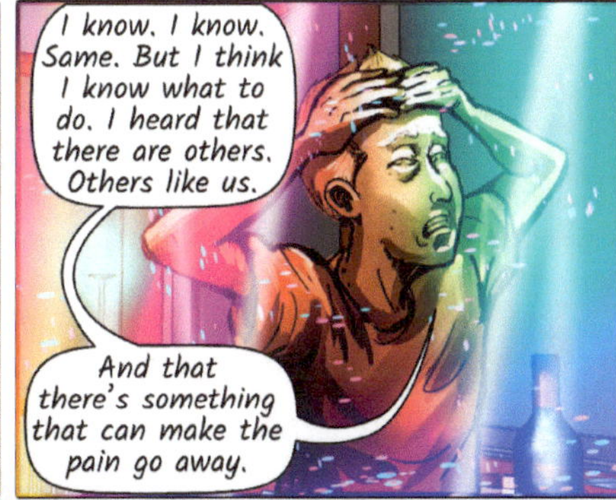

I know. I know. Same. But I think I know what to do. I heard that there are others. Others like us.
And that there's something that can make the pain go away.

EXIT
Let's go. Follow me.

Hey. I was told to come here and ask for help.
That you'd know what I was talking about. We're not doing good, at all.

Hey boys. You've come to the right place. Looks like my bat friends found you as well.
No worry. I can help.

Please, now. I'm fucking freaking out. I don't think I can wait any longer.

It's rough, I know. Body sweats... chills... itchy everywhere... stomach cramps... and those thoughts —
like you just want to rip some fucker's neck out. I see you. And yes, I can help.

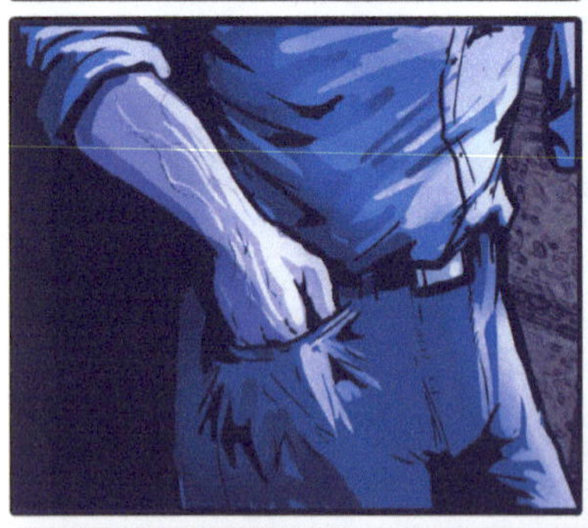

Ahhh... you can sense it. Yes, this will do the trick. Fix you up in no time.
Of course, this shit ain't free. You have cash on you?

I do.
I have
cash.

Here you go. Just take one tab and put it on your tongue.
It just takes a few minutes for the magic to take over.
This should be enough to get you through the next few days.

I'll be around this time tomorrow. Tell your friends.

BOMBASTIC
CLUB

...and I told him no way, it didn't happen like that.
That's so messed up.

Chapter SEVEN

...and then the instructor told the kid to wake up, and the poor kid just kept sitting there, in the middle of the classroom, snoring away.

I finally just reached over and gave him a shove. He woke up, and had no clue what was happening. The class was howling. I felt really bad for him.

Wait, don't tell me... you are now dating him? Was he at least cute?
No dad, I'm not dating him. But yes, he did buy me a coffee after class.

HAHAHAHA
HAHAHAHA
HEEHEEHEE

Aha! I knew you weren't all homework and no fun! What about you Linda — are you dating anyone at school?

Actually, I have a boyfriend here in Richland. I met him last summer when I worked out at Hanford.

Of course... who doesn't work out there around here. What's he do out there? Hopefully he's not anywhere near those tanks.

Actually... he is out at the Tank Farms — but more of a Security Officer role.
Sorry, I know this is a touchy subject with my mom, and her history out there. Also, with what you guys went through with Jared.

Well, everyone has to make a living somehow! Nothing personal, believe me.
I talk to people all day long every day at the restaurant who either work out there, or their family works out there.

We live on a multi-billion-dollar nuclear clean-up site after all... sadly, it's everyone's toxic bread and butter.

Changing the subject... anything exciting planned for you girls this weekend, other than sitting here with your elders?

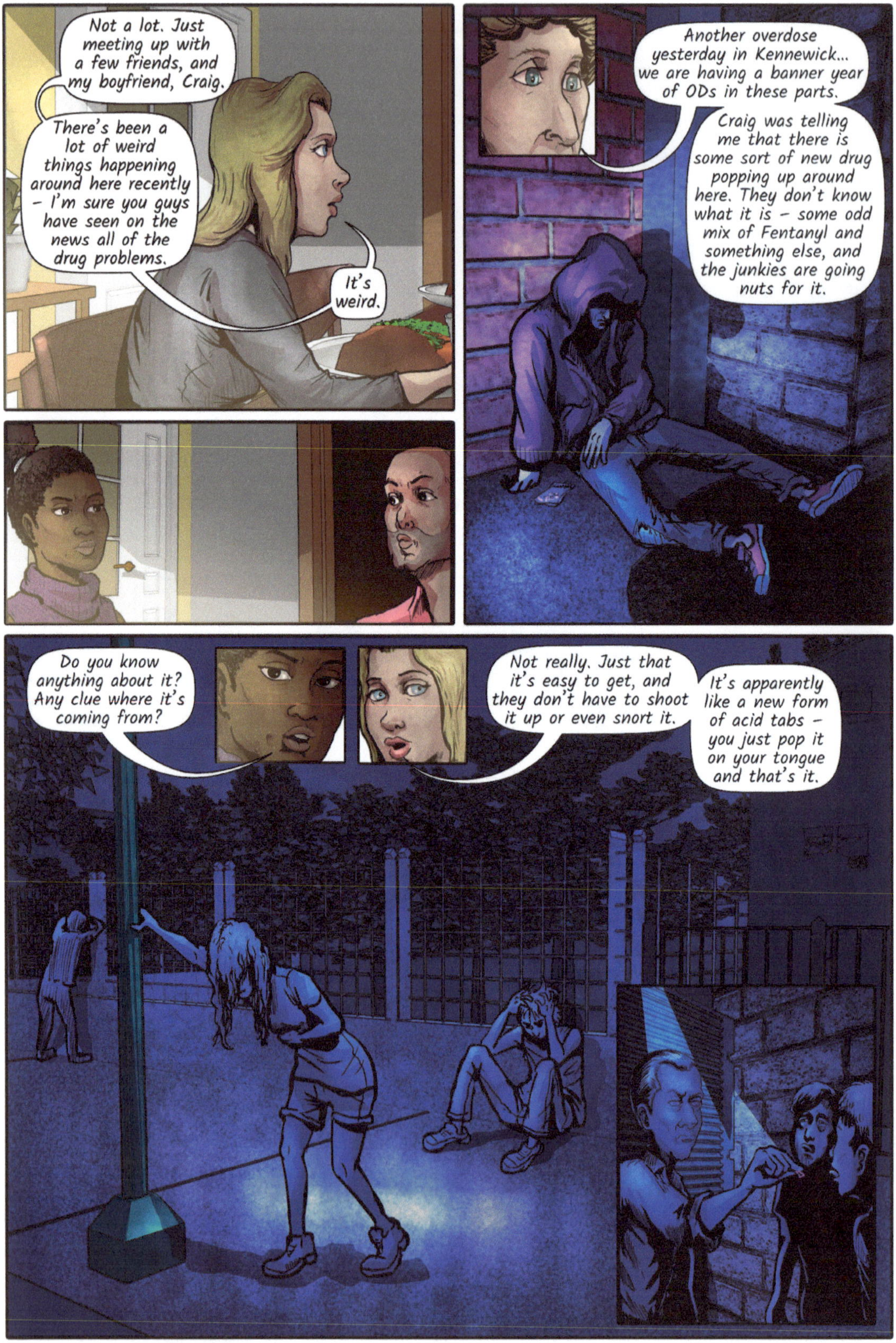

Not a lot. Just meeting up with a few friends, and my boyfriend, Craig.
There's been a lot of weird things happening around here recently – I'm sure you guys have seen on the news all of the drug problems.
It's weird.

Another overdose yesterday in Kennewick... we are having a banner year of ODs in these parts.
Craig was telling me that there is some sort of new drug popping up around here. They don't know what it is – some odd mix of Fentanyl and something else, and the junkies are going nuts for it.

Do you know anything about it? Any clue where it's coming from?
Not really. Just that it's easy to get, and they don't have to shoot it up or even snort it.
It's apparently like a new form of acid tabs – you just pop it on your tongue and that's it.

Well, your mom knows this — but between us, that is why Ali is here this weekend.
I'm worried about her friend Brett.

We had a not-so-kosher boys' night the other night — I studied up on football and everything, words I never thought would come out of this gay mouth.

But he showed up high on something. It was scary. He was all twitchy, and nervous, and, like, sweaty. The kicker was when I saw blood all over his shirt.
When I confronted him on it, he hightailed it out of here. So I called in the leading expert in crisis management — namely, my genius daughter and detective Ali, to come and talk to him. See what's going on.

I hope it's nothing. Especially not some new fucked up acid tab that's killing people around here.

He seems too smart for that. But...his girlfriend Shannon is on the East Coast, he's working full time out at Hanford, and taking classes at the community college...

so who knows what he's doing around here in his spare time, if he has any.

Poor guy. He's such a sweetheart. He was really helpful to me during my own whistleblower nightmare last year.
I'm hoping the best for him. When are you seeing him Ali?

Good question. I've called a bunch of times... left some messages. No response, which is weird for him.
I'm afraid I'm going to have to go out and find him. But I have to admit I'm not sure where to go.

Linda... any clue where 19-year-old Richlanders are hanging these days?
I'm meeting Craig and his friends later at some new all-ages club called Bombastic. You should come with me. I can help you look for Brett.

Sounds like you two ladies are hitting the town. Jennifer... wanna stay and make it a movie night with me?
No booze but I promise loads of show tunes and popcorn and treats. Or, as I call it, a normal Friday night.

I couldn't think of a better way to spend my Friday night. Deal. You ladies be safe.
Beware of the Richland usual suspects – witches, ghosts, and now, it seems, drug addled tweakers.

CLAP

Chapter EIGHT

BOMBASTIC
CLUB

Hey you. Come outside with me? It's too loud in here.

Hi there. It's been a few months.
How are you doing? Missing Shannon?

I... um...
I'm good.
Really good.
Good to see you.

Brett, I tried calling you and left a bunch of texts this week. I never heard back. What's up?
Ah shit, I lost my phone. I need a new one.

You actually don't have a phone? Does that even happen?
Brett, what's going on with you?

What? Nothing. Nothing's going on with me. I'm just, you know, working, studying. That's it.

Well, you look like shit.
Thanks.

My dad told me about last weekend. He had been looking forward to hanging out with you, seeing you.
And you showed up obviously wasted or on something, and all bloody? Brett, what is happening with you? Why were you bloody?

Bloody? Was I? I don't know, I...

Sniff
Sniff

Okay, enough bullshit. You know me — nothing gets past me.
Have you talked to Shannon lately? Does she know what's up with you?

BASTIC
CLUB

Brett, you're obviously on something. I'm not judging — I'm here to help you. I won't even tell Shannon.
I know what's going on around here — in Richland — this new drug everyone is doing — and many are dying from. Are you on it too?

Brett, are you on Fentanyl? How did this even start? Where do you get –

Ali, stop. Just stop. I'm not on Fentanyl.
At least I don't think I am. I don't know what I'm on.
But... you are on something?

Okay, okay, fuck, yes, I'm on something. Or I need to be soon.
Something happened to me Ali
– something bad – before I went to your dad's house.
... the blood?

Yes, the blood. Don't look at me like that – it was my blood, not someone else's.
Oh shit, I can't do this. I can't tell you.

Brett, look what we've gone through together over the past few years. Witches. Ouija Boards, ghosts, seances.
And we came out ahead. You can tell me. I won't tell my Dad, or Shannon. Let me help you. Who hurt you that night?

BOMBASTIC CLUB

Brett, what? What is happening?

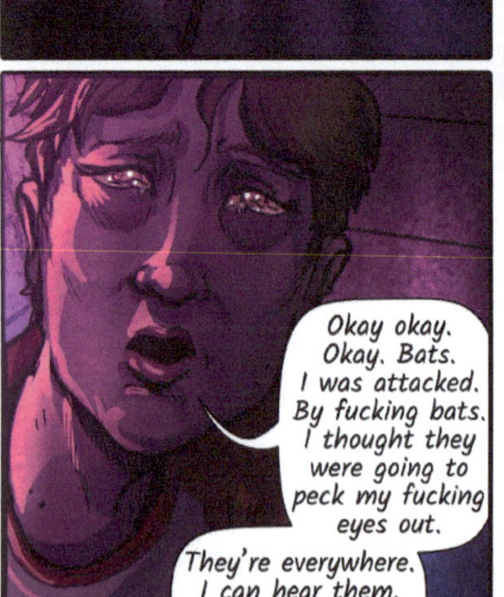

Okay okay. Okay. Bats. I was attacked. By fucking bats. I thought they were going to peck my fucking eyes out.
They're everywhere. I can hear them. Can you see them? Hear them?

Brett, there are no bats here.
What are you talking about?

I bought a pizza for me and your dad. And in the parking lot – these bats – they attacked me. Bit me.
You got attacked by bats? Then what happened?

I don't know... I got up. There was blood everywhere
And that's when it started. I started feeling... weird.
Weird, how?

Just kind of sick. I feel it now. Like I'm going to die. My body itches. I feel sick to my stomach. And there's more. I ... I...
You what? Tell me, I can help you.

I get these urges. Like, violent urges. That I need something. To feel better.
And when I'm around certain people...I can smell it. Whatever it is I need. And I just want to like rip into them.

So...are you like, a vampire? Do you bite people? Do you drink people's blood.
No! I'm not a vampire. And no, I don't bite people. But there's a man. A man who gives us what we need.
I think I even saw his face when the bats were on me.

A man. Like Dracula?

No Ali, not like Dracula. Just this guy. He was there.
And now I see him around.
Here.
Around here.

Like here here? Is he here now?
Yes, here. He'll be here later. There are more of us. Like me.

Wait, more of you who were bitten by bats?
What are you telling me right now?

Ali, I don't know. All I know is that there are more of us.
And we buy something from him. Something that makes the pain and urges go away.
Like, drugs? He sells you guys drugs? What kind of drugs?

I don't know. It's like an acid tablet.
We just put it on our tongue and within seconds the pain goes away ... and we feel better - for a while at least.
But then it comes back - a few hours later, or like the next day, even worse than before. Like now. I feel like I'm going to die.

You were bitten by bats. You've felt sick ever since. Some guy was there, and now that guy is selling you and others some fucking acid dose to make it go away.
Wait, do you smell me differently? What are you sniffing for?
What does that even mean?

No. I don't know. I don't smell it on you. But I never know. There are many people around here who smell a certain way — and when I get near them my body starts really freaking out.
Until I get the dose. And then I'm good. For a while. I can't explain. It's messed up.

For fuck's sake this town is literally the most fucked up town on this planet.
Oh really?

Sniff
Sniff

Are those your bat friends?
Ali, I'm sorry. I don't know what's happening. I think there are a bunch of us who were bitten.
But I also think there are others who are just taking the dose, and are now hooked.
Look, I have to go. I'll call you tomorrow.

Wait, Brett, don't go. Let me go with you.
Ali, stay out of this.
I know you, always snooping your way into things. This is dangerous.

Wait, one more question. The smelling. I still don't get it. Where is it the worst?
Around here, where do you catch this smell you're talking about?

Definitely out there. When I'm at work. At Hanford. When I get there, I feel better.
And my nose goes into like spaz overload. Ali, I gotta split. Stay out of this – it's not safe.

BOMBASTIC
CLUB

I thought I lost you! Did you find your friend?

What? Oh, yeah.
I did. I talked to him. I... I am not sure what's happening.
But I need to fix this.

Hey Ali gurl, what's up? Wanna dance?

And who's this pretty lady?
Oh, this is my friend, Linda.
Linda, Brett.

Hey Brett, nice to meet you.
Looks like you're having a good night.
Yes it does. Brett... you're so high. Let me take you home.

What? No way Ali, I'm staying. Come on, it's a party. Stay. Dance. Have fun. Linda, wanna dance?
No thanks, my boyfriend is here. Ali, I'll catch you later. Are you good here?

Really?
Is anyone good here?

I'm heading home.

The
Spudnut
Shack
Chapter NINE

Well good morning. And welcome to the Spudnut Shack. I'm your host, Van.
Please enjoy a fresh-baked Spudnut on me. Take the chocolate one – they're the best.

All right ladies – let us live vicariously through you.
How was your night on the town, here in Witchland Snitchland Twitchland? Ali, did you find Brett?

Our night out was... interesting.
And yes, I found Brett. Or least some strange version of Brett I didn't recognize whatsoever.
Well thank the Lord he's still alive. How was he?

He's...a hot mess.
A hot... sober mess? Or just a hot messy mess?
Definitely the latter.
Do you think it's drugs?
I hope it's not that new drug we were talking about.

Ummm...he's definitely got a problem.
I talked to him before he dosed — which, Dad, is probably how he was when you saw him — and afterwards, which is when Linda met him last night.

Yes, he was definitely on something.

There's more to it than just a drug problem. Something crazy is happening around...

Sniff Sniff

What the hell are you doing girl? Sniffing at me?
If you want to know what cologne I'm wearing, it's Versace.
Probably not a word you hear around here often.

The Spudnut Shack

Well, I have to tell you – that's not the first time this has happened this week.
These kids are fucking freaking out... and it's fucking freaking the shit out of me.

That's what I was about to say. There's something else going on here. Yes, there is some fucked-up drug hitting these streets.
But...and I hate to say it... But once again, I think it's somehow related to...

Oh for fuck's sake. Don't tell me it's related to Hanford.
Now what trauma is Hanford causing?
Hundreds of deaths and countless cases of cancer aren't enough?
Well duh, of course it is.

Okay, nobody freak out. Dad, that means you.
Can you promise me you will just calmly listen, and not like jump up and down and scream and lose your shit?

Girl, like I ever...

Okay, here goes. We are dealing with bats. Fucked-up bats. That bite.

Okay, I'm calm.
So, vampires walk among us?
Here in Richland?
Oh my God, Dad calm down. No, vampires do not walk among us.
But there are bats. Biting people.
That's where Brett's blood came from.

I knew it. He kept like sniffing me and looking like he was going to lunge at my throat.
Brett's a vampire. Brett's a fucking vampire.
Nosferatu. Brett.
Van, honey, let Ali speak.

Thanks. So, yes, there's a bat problem. And it makes people freak out.
And, it would appear, the only thing that can cure this is a drug. This new wonder drug. That some mystery man is selling.

HEEEEEEE

Is he... Count Dracula? Maybe Lestat?

HEHE

I don't know who he is. But I'm going to find out.
Oh Ali gurl that's why I called you here.
Ladies, Ali to the rescue. She's a genius, this one. Oh, and a trail blazer. She'll find a way to fix this bat shit.

Ali, I can't believe you figured this all out just last night.
I told you, she's a genius. A regular Clarice Starling.

Who?

Ignore him.
But yes, I do have a plan. We're going to have to work fast. Fast, as in tonight fast. Are you all free?

Yes, we're free.
Just tell us our mission impossible, Judi Dench.

Linda, you and I are going to the club again tonight. Let's meet early and rehearse.
Say 8:00? But first...
Linda, you are the animal expert. If I were a bat, where would I live around here?

Oh my God. We are being summoned to the Bat Cave.
Holy shit, Clarice.
CLAP CLAP CLAP CLAP
Spudnut Shack

Spudnut Shack

Chapter TEN

Okay, it's go-time.
The cave is right over there.

We've done many trailblazing things together, but this takes the cake.
We're about to gas the shit out of some toxic bats.

Look at us.
Fucking who ya gonna call?

We're sure they're in there? What if it's full of regular bats?

This is our best shot. According to Craig, there aren't a lot of bats out here...
and this seems to be the place they come from, and live.
We have to do this now, while they are sleeping.
How do we know they won't come out and bite us also?

Linda and I researched it — this is the only gas that will do damage to the bats.
It's our best shot. Now, get your masks on.

I'll count down to five with my fingers, then we let it rip.
And whatever you do, don't take off your gas mask until we get back to the car.

I'm ready. Sigourney, how about you?
Let's do this.

FWOOOOOOOOSH

Eeeek
Eeeek
FLAP FLAP FLAP
FLAP
FLAP
Eeek
Eeeek
FLAP FLAP FLAP
FLAP
FLAP
FLAP
Eeek

Let's go.

Ladies, my life is now complete.
We opened some major cans of whoop ass on those fucking toxic vampires. Gurl!

Chapter ELEVEN

Okay, it's now or never. Are you ready?
Just do like we rehearsed.
I think so. Ready as I'll ever be.
Hanging out with you is certainly an adventure.

Hey you. Back at it again, huh?
Not looking so great there Brett. Can I talk to you outside?
EXIT

Ali, you should leave. Just go back to school.
You don't belong here, not in this mess.

Brett, you know I'm here to stop this, and to help you. I think I have a plan to do both. Just let me go with you to meet the dealer.

No way Ali. And I should never have told you any of that shit. Forget it.
I was lying. So I've got a little drug problem. I'll get over it.
Everyone around here dabbles with drugs. No big deal.

Look Brett, you can't take back what you said. And I've been working out a plan to fix all of this.
One phase of the plan was a success – my dad and I killed those fucking bats today. They can't bite anyone else.

What? Ali, you're insane! Don't drag your poor dad into this! And those bats are deadly, for fuck's sake.
This is one dangerous game you are playing here Ali.
EXIT

Ali, I've got to bounce.
I'm not doing too good. I need to go find my friends.

Brett, those people aren't your friends. They are trouble. You guys all need help.
Those drugs are going to kill you. People are dying around here. You could be next.
Let me help you. Let's go to the hospital, now, and get you better.

Ali, just let me go one more time, and then that's it, I promise.
You can help me get better then. I just need my dose now, or I'm going to lose my shit.
Sniff
Sniff

And who do we have here?
I haven't seen you around before.

Hey. I'm just here for my dose. Like everyone else.

Welcome to the club, pretty lady.

Brett, it's not just another drug you're taking. This has something to do with where you work. Hanford.
I don't know the whole connection, but this shit is somehow connected to that place. It's dangerous.
We need to get you checked into a hospital and looked at. Come with me now. I'll take you. Do it for yourself...for Shannon.

I will, I promise. But not tonight.
I need one more dose.
Tomorrow.
Find me tomorrow.

Got it.
Let's go.
Nice job.
God I hope
Brett's
alright.

The
Spudnut
Shack
The
Spudnut
Shack
Chapter TWELVE

Here we are again, brunching at the finest establishment in this shitty town.

I wish I had some bubbles to offer, and maybe a Croque Monsieur or something, but Sunday is Salted Caramel Cinnamon Bun Day.
My idea.
They're delicious...and a hit as you can see.

All right ladies, talk. I think our exterminator field trip was a success
— I still can't believe we did that — but how did the night go?
I think it was a success. Linda here is a regular Meryl Streep.
She twitched her way to a baggie of mystery drugs.

It's a sad day when I'm happy and proud of my daughter for successfully buying drugs in an alley, pretending to be a junkie.
Well, it worked. I have them here with me. Ali, now what?

Dad...it's on you now. I see your cop friends are here. Are you ready for this?

Every Sunday,
like clockwork.
These cops love
their donuts.

Must be
the salted
caramel.

Or maybe they
are enthralled by
the hot manager.
Spudnut Shack
By that,
I mean
me.

Yes, I'm ready.
The tall drink of
water is the
police chief.
Believe it or not
we are friends.
Girl, slide me
over those drugs
and let me do
my thang.

Wish Daddy luck as he offers drugs to our police chief.

Zoinkers team, that's that. Another mystery solved – hopefully – by Ali Doo and her scrappy ragtag posse.
I'm hoping that little baggie of doom goes right into the labs for testing – my big strapping Police Chief promised it would.

Nice job Dad. You get better and better at this intrigue shit all the time.
A regular Jessica Fletcher you are.

Who's Jessica Fletch-

Never mind. He's obsessed with watching Murder She Wrote reruns. Linda, it's on Craig now – is he all set?
Yes. He's been watching footage on security cams, covertly asking around out there about anyone acting strangely.

I think my description of him is pretty detailed. Craig thinks he knows who he is.
Hopefully this all ends soon.

Welcome to Hanford
WHERE SAFETY COMES FIRST
...Later that night...

He's here. He's out there.
Be careful. He's fucking scary.

Alright, he's out there, by the tanks. Let's proceed cautiously. He's a live wire.

Tom Jenkins!
Slowly stand up and turn around with your hands up.

SPLASH

Chapter THIRTEEN

Hey honey, how you doing? You made it back to school okay?
Well that's good. No, no sign of Brett. I'm worried sick. I talked to his parents, they haven't seen him either for a few days.
What about Shannon, has she heard from him? We just have to pray he's okay.

What? They arrested him? How'd you hear that?
Well, it must be nice dating a security officer out at the most toxic worksite on the planet.

I can't believe he was selling that toxic shit to kids. Just another feather in the cap of this shit show town.
Hope he goes to prison for life. Thank God Craig caught him in the act.
I hope this can be put behind us now.

No, it doesn't change the fentanyl problem, but it does change the toxic waste acid tab and toxic bat problem.

104

Leave it to my gurl Ali to crack the whole case open in 48 hours. Damn girl, you never cease to amaze me.
No, I haven't seen any of those crazies in the restaurant in a few days — a good sign I hope.

AAAH!

Ali honey, I have to go. Brett's here. Of course he scared the piss out of me again.
But at least he's here! I'll call you later.

Oh thank Jesus Brett you are alive! You had us all worried sick!

Van...I need help. Please, help me.
Of course. Let's go to the hospital now.

Hello, 911? I ... we... need help. Please send help.

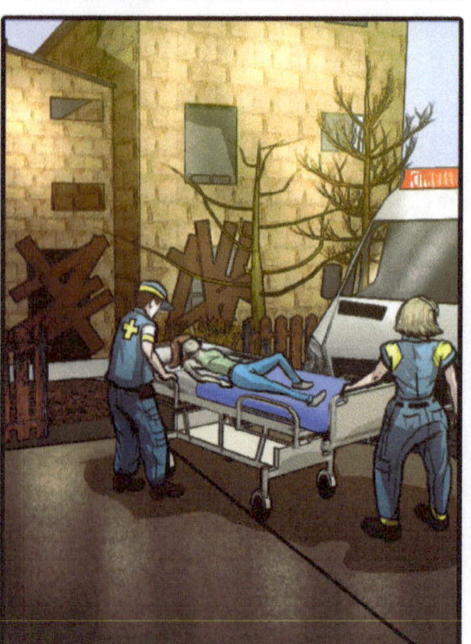

RICHLAND MEMORIAL HOSPITAL

Chapter FOURTEEN

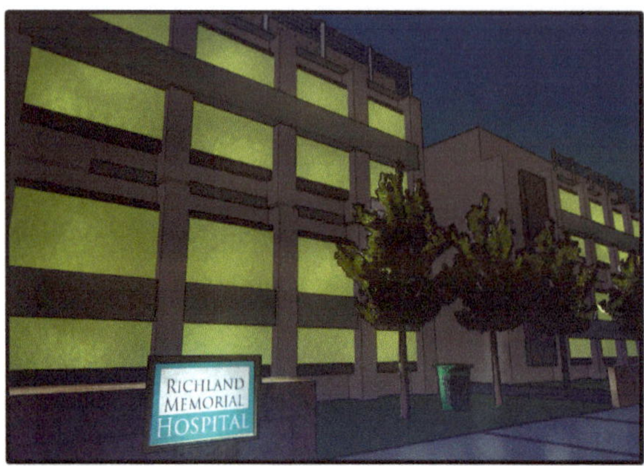

RICHLAND
MEMORIAL
HOSPITAL

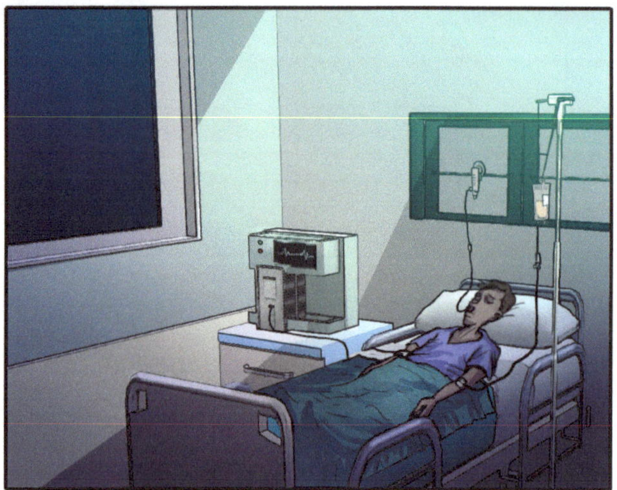
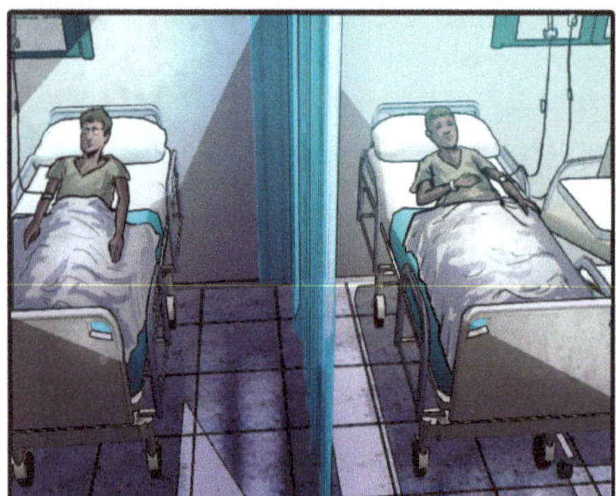

Hey you... it's just us.

And look — I brought spudnuts! You can share them with your friend here.

Thanks Van... you're the best.

Hi Brett. Looking better!
We talked to the doctor — sounds like the blood transfusion was a success.

For you as well?

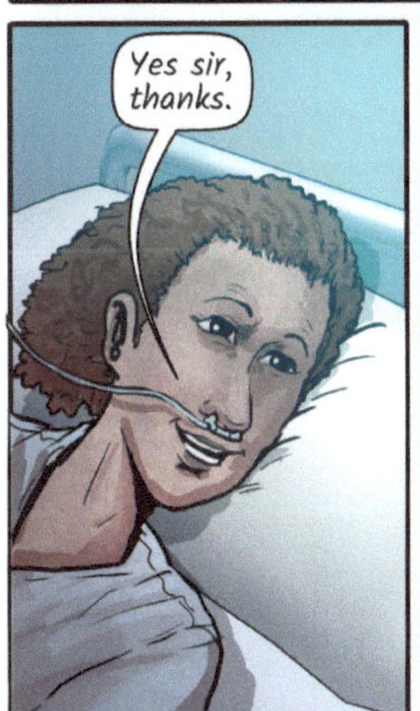

Yes sir, thanks.

Ali of course sends her love. I'm sure you've spoken with Shannon.
We all just want you better, take whatever time you need to heal, and get over this nightmare.
The Spudnut Shack

Hey, is it true you two like took down those fucking bats? That's rad.

I'll give my superhero daughter the credit. Nothing in this town can take her down. Brett, we should go. I'll come back tomorrow. Get some rest.
Both of you.
Thanks Van. And Jennifer. I really appreciate all that you've done. See you tomorrow.

Watch the moon tonight — they say it's gonna be a full one!

YAWN

Owoooooooo
Owoooooooo
Owoooooo
Owooooooo
Owoooo
Owoooooo
Owooooooo
Owoooooo
Owoooooooo
Owoooooooo
RICHLAND MEMORIAL HOSPITAL